The White Wolf and Seven Spirits

A Boy's Vision Quest

Tracy Vallier

Tracy Vallier

Illustrations by Daniel A. Vallier

Orders:

Tracy Vallier
P.O. Box 14097
South Lake Tahoe, California 96151
(or) sevendevilsbook@gmail.com

Cover and text design: Jonathan Gullery
Back cover illustration: Daniel A. Vallier
Front cover photograph: Monte Vallier

Printed by RJ Communications in the United States of America

ISBN: 978-0-9815067-3-9

DEDICATION

*To children
of all ages who seek their destinies*

CONTENTS

ALONG THE WESTERN SLOPE

For several days I've been mapping rock formations and faults along the steep western slope of the Seven Devils Mountains in Idaho, far above the Snake River in Hells Canyon. It has been a particularly tough day with a long and hot afternoon climb of more than two thousand feet. I glance at my watch. It's six o'clock and early evening. I left camp at seven that morning and descended two thousand feet before following the Granite Creek Fault for more than a mile. The fault apparently moved sometime in the last ten thousand years and it could move again with devastating results.

I look down at my clothes and deeply tanned arms. A long rip down the right leg of my Levi's pants and two jagged scratches along the right forearm remind me of a fall that morning when a tree root reached out and grabbed my worn Redwing boots. I stumbled and fell, then bounced and slid down a steep talus slope before finally stopping, ripping the denim pants and gouging gashes on my arm during the slide. I stopped sliding just before tumbling over a precipice several hundred feet high. Once again I had challenged fate and won.

I lean on the handle of my four-pound hammer and rest, reflecting back on the more than forty years of field work spent in western Idaho and eastern Oregon, mostly in Hells Canyon and the Seven Devils Mountains where I've been unraveling the mysteries of the region's geologic history.

Hard days like this make me realize that my time in this steep and rugged terrain is coming to an end. I'm too old to follow this all-consuming passion much longer.

I walk into the primitive campsite, lay my green daypack, hammer, notebook and map case on the ground and slump into an aluminum-folding chair that I'd backpacked in with other equipment and food. The chair is my only luxury. I take off a well-worn straw hat and wipe sweat from my face with a faded red handkerchief. I take the Brunton compass from a leather case on my belt and open it. I stare into the mirror to see three new scratches across my right cheek. I stroke my gray beard with extended fingers.

I dig into the daypack, bring out an aluminum canteen of tepid water and drink the remaining few swallows while pondering the task of preparing dinner. I scratch my head and think: *The food I carried in five days ago is running low and I'll have to return to the trailhead at Windy Saddle within the next two or three days and drive to Riggins or Grangeville for more supplies. I'd better catch a fish or two tonight for dinner.*

I look around the small tree-enclosed campsite and notice that a few pieces of firewood remain. I hadn't burned it all during the long writing session the night before when I sat on the aluminum chair, within light cast by the campfire, and wrote most of a short story about an apparition I'd encountered at the Temperance Creek cabin more than thirty years earlier.

I have no tent. Good weather encourages me to sleep on the ground where I can hear the slightest rustle of an animal's movements and feel the cooling breeze of an approaching storm. Natural odors in a grove of fir and pine trees wake a dormant primitive spirit. I'm at peace in these surroundings. It had rained two evenings before and I, well accustomed to the vagaries of weather in the mountains and canyons of eastern Oregon and western Idaho, had huddled under an Army poncho similar to those issued to soldiers during the Vietnam War and slept with my back against the trunk of a pine tree.

I'm camped on a ridge along the north side of Granite Creek canyon, about thirty yards from the turbulent stream. I listen to water bouncing through the verdant canyon as it hurtles toward Snake River. The stream's noises are soothing and I nod off into a light sleep. When I wake early evening has turned into dusk. The faint glow from a rising full moon touches sharp peaks of the Seven Devils Mountains that tower above me.

I light a small pile of twigs in the fire ring with a match and throw on larger branches. Flames give off showers of sparks as sap heats and bursts. I wait until the flames subside and grab a fishing rod, empty canteens, and chair and step slowly down the slope to Granite Creek. A cramp in my left calf stops me and I rest for a minute or so before continuing. I walk along the stream, pushing tree branches aside until I arrive at a deep pool below a cascading waterfall. The roar of plunging water drowns out all other noise. I set up the chair, fill a canteen with cold water and drink the entire quart without stopping to breathe. I fill both canteens and set them on the stream's bank. I sit on the chair and lazily throw in the line; it has a small bobber attached with a lure fastened below it. The bobber floats into the current and I lose sight of it in the approaching darkness. My mind wanders as I reflect on the day's accomplishments.

The moon meanders over a mountain peak and fills the narrow canyon with its reflected rays. I stand up, reel in the bobber and lure and take them off the line. I tie a lead weight and number-ten hook to the line and take a grasshopper from my shirt pocket that I caught during the afternoon climb. I put the grasshopper on the hook, being careful to completely cover the sharp barb.

The fishing rod glistens in the moonlight as I cast the grasshopper into rippling water. The bait drifts downstream and I reel it in to try again. I step back from the bank because moonlight is throwing my shadow onto the water. The bait is cast again and it flies most of the way across the pool. I slowly reel it in. A shadowy form follows the bait. I cast again, this time toward the middle of the pool, and a thick arc of silver jumps into the air as the grasshopper-baited hook nears water. A fish grabs the bait and falls back into the water pulling the line deep beneath the pool's surface. I let out more line as the fish dives and then slowly reel it in. The fish jumps out of the water, trying to dislodge the hook that grips its jaw. We work against each other in an ancient dance of life and death, but the fish finally tires. I reel in my worthy opponent, a fifteen-inch trout, seize it behind the gills with thumb and fingers and hit it over the head with a stick to make a quick kill. I wrestle the hook from its jaw and gut the fish, throwing entrails and head into the pool for other fish to devour.

I look up at the moon, raise a fist into the air and shout, "Ee-yah, no freeze-dried stew tonight." My mouth waters as I think about the succulent meat.

I carry the chair, rod, canteens and trout up the steep bank and return to the fire. I take an aluminum skillet from the large backpack, along with a small plastic bottle of cooking oil, place two stream-rounded rocks along one side of the fire ring and scrape burning embers between them. I cut the trout into quarters to fit in the skillet. The skillet sits flat on the rocks and I feed more sticks into the fire under it. I pour in cooking oil and carefully lay the fish in the sizzling oil.

From experience I know that one minute on a side is enough to cook a trout in a hot skillet. I look at my watch and turn the pieces over with a hunting knife after one minute. Hot oil spatters on my arm. Another minute passes, but I leave the fish quarters frying for an extra fifteen seconds because of their sizes. I pull the red handkerchief from a back pocket, wrap it around my right hand, take the hot skillet off the rocks and put it on the ground to cool. I unfold the aluminum chair, sit down, reach into the backpack and bring out a packet of saltine crackers. I dip a cracker into the fish-flavored oil.

I raise the cracker to my mouth and stop. An unexpected noise comes from somewhere within the bushes and trees east of the campsite. My eyes search the undergrowth for movement, but there is none. I toss the cracker into my mouth and reach for the skillet of fried fish.

EL VIEJO ARRIVES

Expectations for an uneventful evening are shattered by a voice from the shadows. "May I join you?"

I jump from the chair, grab my hammer as a weapon, and look into the depths of the forest. I see nothing. I raise the hammer and ask, "Who's there? Come out so I can see you."

"Those are appropriate questions. Have no fear because I'm not here to harm you." His words sag under a thick Spanish accent.

I still can't see him, although slight movements far back in the bushes indicate his presence. He approaches the campsite, still in the shadows.

He asks, "May I eat some of your fish?"

I hesitate for several seconds and then say, "You're very welcome to the fish." I put the hammer on a nearby rock where I can reach it.

A frail old man walks into the fire's dim light wrapped in a brown blanket. He is stooped over from either pain or age and walks slowly to the fire. He sits on the aluminum chair and crosses his legs. Tight leather moccasins protrude from faded denim pants. The blanket slips off his shoulders; he has a pink bandana around his neck and wears a yellow sleeveless undershirt with *BE HAPPY* spelled out in bold letters across the front. Long silver hair is tied in a ponytail. But, it's the old man's face that captures most of my attention and interest. His eyes sink far back into a dented skull and a hooked nose hangs down to mouth level. Face wrinkles are set in deep rhombic lines, arranged so neatly that it seems the lines had been cut there. His mouth is caved in and contains few, if any, teeth. I stare at his shoulders; across both shoulders long white scars stand out in stark contrast to his brown skin.

I ask, "You are hungry?"

"Si—yes. I've traveled far."

I pass him the skillet. "Eat all you want. I can catch another fish if it's needed. Be careful though, the skillet is still hot."

"Gracias—thank you." He takes the skillet from me. I hand him six saltine crackers and he nods his head.

The old man pulls the backbone and ribs from the largest fish quarter and begins eating by holding the fish in his hand. He throws the bones into the fire. Meanwhile, his eyes probe mine. I cannot look away and stare into his eyes. The irises are a pale charcoal gray with vertical yellow slices. Black pupils seem bottomless and reflections of the flames leap across their surfaces.

He notices that I'm staring and mutters, "Eyes show the strength of one's soul."

I turn away and look into the fire. Chills finger up my back awakening a dim memory. I had seen those eyes before. But, where had I seen them? I shake my head to clear it.

He finishes eating two fish quarters and returns the skillet. I pick up a piece of fish and chew on it, all the while watching the specter as he takes a yellow pipe out of a brown leather purse that hangs from a braided leather belt. The pipe's curved black stem shines like polished ebony. He fills the pipe with tobacco from the purse and lights it with a small burning branch, sucking in the smoke and letting it drift out slowly through distended nostrils.

"Sit down there," he demands, and points to a spot directly across the fire. He hands me the pipe. "Smoke."

I sit on the ground, suck in, and inhale smoke from the old man's pipe. The taste fills my throat with a peculiar sweetness. I hand the pipe back and it leaps to his mouth. His nose hangs down and nearly buries its tip inside the pipe's bowl.

I ask, "Who are you and where do you live?"

"I live in a place far from here."

"Who are you?"

The end of his ponytail is draped over a shoulder. "I have many names."

"What should I call you?"

"You give me a name."

I put another branch on the fire as I ponder his statement. "Okay," I say, "I'll give you a name. You're a very old man and wisdom clothes you like a well-tailored suit. In Mexico and other parts of Latin America wise old men are called 'El Viejo.' May I call you Viejo?"

"I like that name and I've been called that before." He hesitates and whispers, "It was a long time ago."

He hands me the pipe and I fill my lungs. I hand it back over the fire.

I ask, "How did you get here? And why are you here, so far from any town and the comforts you would find there?"

"I came on the back of a great eagle and am here to talk with you." The old man scratches his head and flakes of dandruff cascade from his fingertips. His eyes meet mine. "I know you well and have watched you for years as you toiled in Hells Canyon and in the bordering Seven Devils Mountains."

I shiver from a sudden chill and scoot closer to the fire for warmth. "Why have you done that?"

He sucks on the pipe and watches the smoke curl above the fire ring. "You have a decision to make because your age will not let you work in the canyon and mountains much longer." He hesitates and then says, "You are an old man."

My mind jumps from children to spouse to career as I try to figure out what he means. "Decision? What decision?"

"You will make a decision soon about the rest of your life. I don't know what you'll decide, but I'm here to help."

"I'm in a quandary about what you mean, Viejo."

He puffs several times on the pipe. The sweet aroma of his tobacco mixes with the harsh odor of burning tree branches. I toss several more branches into the flames. Sparks rise and the flames make dark shadows appear among nearby trees and bushes. The full moon is nearly overhead by now and casts its own shadows on the rugged landscape. The rush of water in Granite Creek subsides into a distant rumble and forest stillness descends to enfold us. A branch falls from a nearby tree and my shoulders jerk in surprise. I sit down on the ground.

El Viejo squints across the fire. "When you make the decision you'll be swimming in a strong current that will carry you to places you have never dared to dream about. Vaya— go with curiosity and deep gratitude to the Great Spirit."

He hands the pipe across the fire and I suck in smoke as I ponder his words. I become slightly dizzy. A green branch pops in the fire as it gives up moisture. Noise from the creek's plunging waters once again fills the narrow canyon and chases away the temporary tranquility. I stand up and give back the pipe. He knocks the bowl against his hand and fills it with fresh tobacco. I put another branch on the fire and lean against a tree trunk where I can see his eyes reflecting the flames.

I stretch and say, "I've thought much about what I want to do, but I'm afraid age and health will keep me from putting my thoughts into action. Maybe they're only dreams. Perhaps, I tell myself, I should spend what little time I have left with the ones I love." I move from the tree and sit on the ground across the fire from El Viejo. "Anyway, Viejo, I'm afraid to make a decision that will greatly change my life."

The old man looks into the fire for a long time and I think that he will not speak.

Finally, in very clear English he says, "Your family members can get along well without you. In fact, you'll become a burden as you age and weaken. Don't be afraid to follow your dreams, even at your age. People are capable at any time in their lives to follow dreams that inspire them. You have proven that love and responsibility to family need not interfere with your work. You have spent more than forty years pursuing studies of Hells Canyon, the oceans, and island chains that rim the Pacific Ocean. The studies of the rocks and geologic evolution of Hells Canyon and the Seven Devils Mountains are a large part of your destiny. But, there is another component, an ever-lingering component that has been with you for a long time, and you must heed its call."

He stops for a few seconds, takes a deep pull on the pipe and lets smoke out slowly through his nostrils and mouth. "You must remember that there is only one thing that makes a dream impossible to achieve."

"And what is that, Viejo?"

"It is the fear of failure."

Smoke from his pipe swirls around our heads. He closes his eyes and nods. He leans over as if to fall into the fire, but rights himself at the last moment. He looks at me and grins, his upper two canines the only teeth left in a shrunken jaw. He turns and gazes at the peaks of the Seven Devils Mountains, now bathed in moonlight. Among the peaks small patches of snow, left over from winter, sparkle in frozen brilliance. A slight breeze wakes the fire and sparks leap skyward.

Suddenly, the old man turns toward me. He raises both white eyebrows and his eyes open wide. He smiles and says, "I know these mountains well."

"How is that possible? I've never seen you in these mountains."

"I was in these mountains long before your time. In fact, I am really a part of them."

"The Seven Devils?"

"Si—yes, I am part of the Seven Devils Mountains."

I look at him and ask, "How can that be?"

"Believe me. Soon, you also will believe."

He gives me the pipe and I puff on it, this time being

careful not to inhale. I nod in gratitude as I hand it back over the flames. He smiles again. Another branch pops in the fire and flames shoot up into the space that separates us. In the distance a coyote calls to its mate. Farther away the mate answers. A slight breeze fans the fire and flames are swept to one side.

"I'm curious, Viejo. You said that you've been part of the Seven Devils Mountains since long before my time. Can you tell me how they were named? I've heard the Nez Perce story about the Coyote and seven monsters, but I'm really not very satisfied with that explanation."

The wizened old man picks up a branch and throws it into the fire. Sparks explode. The flames flare up again and shadows play hide and seek behind him. He takes the pipe from his mouth, pounds the ashes into the palm of his hand, stares at the ashes for a few seconds, throws them into the fire and watches closely as they disappear in the flames.

He whispers, "The native people you call Indians named the mountains 'Tama Sorna,' which means 'Seven Spirits.' The invading white men translated 'spirits' into 'devils' and that is how the mountains were named."

"Why did the Indians name the mountains Tama Sorna?"

El Viejo gazes into the fire for more than a minute and then glances at peaks in the Seven Devils Mountains where He Devil and She Devil are now bathed in brilliant moonlight. He answers, "It's a story about a young boy who went into these mountains to experience a vision that would help him discover his destiny. When the boy returned home he told the village elders about a vision that involved seven spirits and the elders named the mountain range Tama Sorna."

"Do you remember the story?"

"Si—yes, very well."

"Please tell it to me."

The old man yawns and stretches. "It will take much time to tell."

"I'm not tired."

El Viejo refills the pipe, gingerly picks up a flaming twig from the fire and lights the tobacco. He sucks smoke way down into his bowels; when he exhales the smoke circles his head and obscures it.

I throw more branches on the fire and then sit on the ground with my back against a large smooth rock.

The smoke clears and El Viejo begins telling the story. "Young Indian boys were forced to go into the wilderness to have a vision that would reveal their destinies and guide them throughout their lives. This story is about a boy who had his vision in what are now the Seven Devils Mountains."

The voice of this mysterious old man merges with the partly muted sounds of the crackling fire, rushing stream and howling coyotes. I close my eyes part way and focus all of my attention on the magical story that he tells.

Nee Wahee's Journey Begins

It was a long time ago, long before white men invaded to conquer the native peoples of this country. A chief's son reached the age of twelve winters and it was time for him to become a young man and a warrior. Every boy in the village stayed in the wilderness for many days to have a vision that would serve as a guide to his destiny. Sometimes, the visions were extraordinary and several of the boys were renamed after relating their visions to a council of village elders.

For example, the boy's father, chief of the village, saw a fight between an eagle and a bear in his vision. The bear won and his father was renamed "Bear That Killed Eagle" or "Wahee Na Han Amano" in the native language.

The chief's son was named Little Bear, or "Nee Wahee." The name Nee Wahee, however, was a common name and the boy wanted to be renamed by the elders after having his own spectacular vision, a vision that he would wait for in the wilderness until it came, no matter how long it took.

The boy prepared for the trip with both intoxicating excitement and intense fear—fear that had kept him awake every night since his father said it was time for him to leave home in quest of a vision. Chief Wahee Na Han Amano told Nee Wahee that whatever happened in the wilderness was part of a grand design for his life and the boy could not change what the Great Spirit planned for him.

Nee Wahee thought: *I'll either have a vision of great importance or die in the wilderness. I'll be brave and, if I survive, will become a great warrior with a strong name.*

It was autumn. Leaves were changing colors from green to yellow, orange and red; some were falling from trees. Water in streams had either slowed or dried up and forest animals had eaten most of the berries and fruits. The women and older children were in high meadows gathering tubers of Camas and Balsamroot to dry for winter food. Some men had journeyed to rivers to catch fish that also would be dried and stored for food during the approaching winter. Other men hunted deer and elk.

Chief Wahee Na Han Amano woke Nee Wahee when the sun had not yet peeked over the horizon and led him to the council lodge. They sat on the floor near a fire pit and crossed their legs. Nee Wahee could hear his heart beating as the chief said, "You will leave today in quest of your vision. Take nothing with you except a blanket and the clothes your mother made. Do not return until you've had a worthy vision, one that is appropriate for a future chief. You must grow into a man who can lead our people when I am no longer chief."

The chief lifted his hand and waved toward the door of the lodge, indicating that his son should leave. Nee Wahee felt dizzy as he rose from the ground and walked through the door to go back to his parents' lodge, a house made from tree branches and mud. He looked over the landscape surrounding the village. A light rain had fallen the night before and high hilltops were dusted with the first snow of autumn. He shivered, partly because of a chill in the air, but mostly because he was afraid.

Old men and old women had remained in the village to look after young children who were left behind while women and older children journeyed to high prairies to gather tubers and berries and men fished and hunted. Some old women ground dried Balsamroot tubers between two rocks for making flat bread and most old men smoked long-stemmed pipes, their watery eyes staring into partly forgotten pasts.

Nee Wahee felt a lump growing deep in his chest, making it difficult to breathe. He didn't know where to go for his vision and he certainly didn't want to stay alone at night near wild animals. The boy knew that he might not return home. Several boys had not returned from their vision quests and the whole village mourned their absences, but everyone knew that it was the Great Spirit who decided the outcome of their quests. A bear had killed and eaten his good friend Nee Nanao earlier that summer before he had hiked even one day from the village. The brown bear had a huge hump on its shoulders and was a member of the greatly feared family of bears that often raided camps to drag off children and dogs and to destroy and eat food caches. Nee Wahee shivered when he thought about his mother's screams and wails if he didn't return.

Nee Wahee changed into new deerskin clothes and moccasins that his mother prepared for him and picked up a blanket she made from the softest deerskin. The moccasins and clothes fit loosely because she wanted to leave space for growth. She also fashioned a purse with long leather straps made from an elk's hide. He picked it up. Something heavy was in the purse. He reached inside and found several pieces of flint, some dry twigs, many arm-lengths of fishing or snare line made from beaver guts, and four fishhooks carved from an elk's antler. He smiled in gratitude, knowing that his mother was worried her only son would starve in the wilderness and never return. He put the purse inside his pants so it would not be seen when he left the village.

He looked around the family lodge, his eyes stopping on possessions he loved and would have to leave behind. Early that summer his father made a bow of hardened willow and ten straight arrows of ash for him. Nee Wahee shaped arrowheads from flint and obsidian and tied them onto the shafts with line made from dried guts of weasels and minks. He picked up a tomahawk he made from ash wood and flint, but put it back on the hook knowing that his father would notice if it were missing. He left the bow and arrows in the corner of the lodge.

Nee Wahee combed his long black hair with trembling fingers, reached down into the clay bowls of paints his father had prepared from powdered red and yellow rocks and fish oil, and painted his cheeks, forehead and chin with straight slashes pointing toward his heart. He turned and walked boldly through the door, knowing that when he returned he would be a young man with a spectacular vision, a warrior suitable to be chief in his father's place.

Kano Capoee, the name for "Happy Fish," was leaving on his quest at the same time and they grabbed each other's right arm, held them close together to feel the blood beat in the other's veins, and said in unison, "May the Great Spirit protect and guide you." Kano Capoee turned and walked north and Nee Wahee turned south. Kano Capoee carried a bow and quiver full of arrows. Nee Wahee was tempted to go back for his tomahawk and bow, but he continued walking away from the lodge. His father had said, however, that he must go into the wilderness without them and he always obeyed his father.

Nee Wahee's father was sitting outside the council lodge smoking a long-stemmed pipe, his chiseled face turned toward the rising sun and smoke from the pipe curling into the air above him. Five eagle feathers adorned his head, vivid trophies of killed enemies. He was praying to the Great Spirit who protected the village people from harm and guided their hunts and battles. *Perhaps,* thought Nee Wahee, *he is also praying that I'll return safely.* The boy wanted to tell his father goodbye, but that had been done earlier when the chief motioned for him to leave the council lodge.

Nee Wahee began running on the trail that led away from the village. Tears ran from his eyes, stopping at the slashes of thick paint on his cheeks. His feet pounded against dirt and pebbles on the trail and he was thankful that his mother had sewed an extra strip of deerskin to the moccasins' soles. He stopped and retied the thongs of his moccasins and put the purse over his shoulder. He draped the blanket over his other shoulder and continued running along the trail.

The White Wolf

Tree trunks flashed past as Nee Wahee ran and odors of dry grasses, tree resin and pine cones filtered through his nose. Sunlight met him in openings among tall pine trees and hid from him in shadows. Hairs on his arms stiffened when a branch snapped behind him and he ran faster.

Nee Wahee ran until he came to a massive rock that jutted out and over the trail. He climbed a slope behind the rock and located the cairn of rocks that he had built in late summer. He kneeled to remove the rocks and to uncover a cache of items he buried there. He was surprised to find a bow made from a carefully dried willow branch and seven ash arrows in a roughly sewn deerskin quiver. He hadn't made the bow and arrows and concluded that his father found his small cache of food and had added the weapons. He took out the bow, arrows and quiver and put them on the ground beside his knee. Below them was a knife with a blade made from black and white snowflake obsidian and a handle carved from an elk's antler. He tested the blade's sharpness with a thumb and nodded in satisfaction. The boy stared at the pile of weapons knowing that they would provide him with food and protection. Beneath the bow, arrows, quiver and knife were chunks of flint that he could use to make more arrowheads and the head of a tomahawk. The boy dug farther into the hole and withdrew a bundle of dried tubers of the camas plant and deer jerky, the only items he had put in the cache.

Nee Wahee stood and bowed toward the village. He whispered, "Thank you father for the weapons." He smiled because he realized that all fathers probably provided their sons with weapons for their journeys into the wilderness in search of a vision. Someday, he would do the same for his sons.

Nee Wahee put the food, pieces of flint, and knife in the purse, shouldered the bow and quiver of arrows, climbed down from the massive rock and once again ran along the trail.

Nee Wahee ran and walked for three days. He ate gooseberries, elderberries, grasshoppers, worms and grubs in addition to some of the dried camas tubers and jerky. He slept under his blanket the first two nights with his back against tree trunks. He heard the animals as they performed nightly tasks and listened to leaves falling from tree branches. During the first evening he made a spear shaft from a long and straight branch of a pine tree and carefully chipped a rugged and sharp spear point from a piece of flint. He tied the spear point to the shaft with beaver gut. During the second evening he made the head of a tomahawk from the largest piece of flint and tied it to a forked branch from a young fir tree that he cut off and trimmed with his knife.

The third night he slept on the ground under the blanket with his hands wrapped around the weapons. He slept through the entire night and woke refreshed. A nearby stream gurgled as it rambled through a grove of pine and fir trees and he drank as much water as his stomach would hold.

In the far distance a mountain range reflected morning sunbeams off snow and ice that draped the slopes of jagged peaks. Hunters told stories about terrible demons that lived in those mountains. The hunters stayed away because few large animals were able to live in the harsh landscape, but they were also afraid of the demons.

A branch snapped, bringing Nee Wahee back from the daydreams. He turned and looked back along the trail. A large brown bear with a hump on its shoulders stood upright on a rock near the stream. Nee Wahee grabbed his weapons and thought about his friend Nee Nanao. *Was this the bear that had eaten his friend?* The bear, however, just stared at Nee Wahee, waved a paw toward the distant mountain range and walked into the bushes. The bear's wave was a good omen and Nee Wahee decided that he'd go to those mountains for his vision.

But, Nee Wahee was very hungry. He had eaten most of the jerky and Camas tubers the previous day, and now that he was at higher elevations the berries and fruit were gone from bushes and trees. He decided to save the remainder of the dried food for emergencies, but realized that he would have to find other things to eat. He drank from the stream and began his trek toward the high mountain peaks with his stomach making hunger growls, grunts and squeals.

He crossed a sharp jagged ridge and arrived at another stream when the sun was directly overhead. The boy crawled stealthily along the bank, watching water tumble among rocks and ripple over sand and gravel bars. He hid behind the trunk of a fir tree and watched for fish in a quiet pool of water. Finally, a fish poked out its nose from behind a submerged rock. Nee Wahee waited until the fish swam into the shallows and pounced. He gathered the fish into his arms and carried it to the bank where he peeled the skin off with his teeth and knife and ate the meat raw. The Great Spirit had provided the fish and Nee Wahee bowed toward the sun to thank him.

Nee Wahee, his stomach now full and quiet, sat on the ground and stared at the mountains, which were still far away. He stood, picked up his weapons, quiver and purse, threw the blanket over his shoulder and continued his journey.

He headed toward the peaks. *Perhaps,* he thought, *I'll have a vision if I sit on one of the taller peaks.* He walked steadily for most of the next two days, passing slowly from lowlands to a broad plateau with many streams. He ate the rest of the jerky and camas tubers and slept with his back against the trunks of large trees. He was always hungry and thought often of the food his mother prepared for him in the village. *I'll re-member to thank her for making my clothes and preparing my food after returning from the vision quest. Children, no matter their age, should thank parents for their help and love.*

As Nee Wahee was about to leave the thick forest he saw a yearling deer browsing on bushes near a small stream. He ducked out of sight behind a grove of fir and aspen trees, walked downwind from the deer and crept up on the unsuspecting animal until he was a stone's throw away. He placed the straightest arrow in the bowstring, aimed carefully and shot the unsuspecting animal through the ribs behind its left front leg. The arrow was buried deep into the deer's heart and lungs. The animal hopped three times with blood spurting out along the arrow's shaft and collapsed on the ground. Nee Wahee cut the deer's throat with his knife and blood flowed over the rocks and grass. He cupped a hand under the deer's throat to fill it with blood, lifted it to his mouth and drank.

Nee Wahee raised his bow and knife into the air and screamed, "Ee-yah!" Then he yelled, "Han, han, han," which means "kill, kill, kill." He cut out the arrowhead so as not to break the arrow's shaft, opened the deer's chest with his knife, pulled out the heart and ate it raw, knowing that the strength and courage of the deer would now flow through his body. Blood dripped down his chin and arms and from there onto his chest and legs. Nee Wahee turned to the east toward the spot where the sun had risen that morning and chanted, "tanake ahai supalo," which means "thank you ancestors."

Suddenly, hair on the back of his neck stood up and a chill fingered along his spine. Something or someone was watching. He stepped back into the trees' shadows and his eyes swept the surrounding landscape. He thought: *Could it be a cougar that wants my deer? Could it be a bear? Is it a hunter from another village who will kill me and then steal the deer?*

A large white animal moved among the trees and bushes. It left, however, before Nee Wahee could see it clearly and he waited, searching the forest around him for the animal with his eyes. Something moved behind him and Nee Wahee turned with his spear raised.

A white wolf, a Lonoch Moro, stood on top a rock and stared at him. The wolf was the largest Nee Wahee had ever seen. Its pink tongue dripped saliva onto the rock and its ears pointed straight up. For an instant it looked like the wolf smiled. The eyes were gray and flecked with brilliant yellow colors; the wide pupils were like deep pools of black water. Nee Wahee looked directly into those eyes and said, "Oh Lonoch Moro, please don't kill me. Leave me alone and

I'll share the deer with you." The white wolf looked at the deer's carcass and then at Nee Wahee, bowed its head as if to acknowledge the bargain and trotted off to disappear in a grove of aspen trees.

Nee Wahee turned his back to the wolf. He dragged the deer into a clearing, cut off its head with the tomahawk and obsidian knife and slashed its belly to let the entrails fall on the ground. He pulled the carcass to the other side of the clearing, thereby allowing Lonoch Moro easy access to the head and entrails. He started the long task of skinning. Little by little he stretched the hide and cut the thin layer of fat beneath it. He cut around the hooves and peeled off the hide in two pieces. He wouldn't have time to preserve the hide, so he dragged it to the pile of entrails and left it for the wolf and other animals to eat.

Lonoch Moro watched the boy's activities from within the grove of aspen trees. The wolf's tongue hung out and saliva dripped from his mouth. He raised his nose and sniffed the air.

Nee Wahee gathered a large pile of dead tree branches and made a small pile of dry twigs and moss. He kneeled to start a fire by striking two pieces of flint together over the dry twigs and moss. After several attempts a spark ignited the pile and he blew on it; smoke swirled into his nose making him cough. He fed the fire larger branches until the flames were high.

The boy cut sharp ends on two large and straight branches from a fir tree with his tomahawk to make stakes and pounded them into the ground on each side of the fire with a large rock. He made a drying rack from green aspen branches and tied them together with line made from dried beaver guts. He fastened the rack to the stakes so that it was directly above the fire.

He cut thin strips of meat off the deer's front legs and laid them on the rack to dry over the fire. He took the front legs, with some meat still attached to the bones, and carried them to the clearing where the wolf waited behind a thick fir tree. The wolf swallowed his tongue and his ears stood up again. When Nee Wahee went back to the fire, the wolf began eating the boy's offering of entrails, skin, bones and meat.

All that night, and for the next day and night, Nee Wahee fed the fire and sat near the rack. He put thin strips of deer meat on the rack until the meat dried and then did the whole process over and over again until he had several piles of jerky. He roasted chunks of meat directly over the flames and ate as much as he could, because he knew there would be few animals to kill and eat in the high mountains where he was going. He had to carry all that he would eat because he would be in the snow and wind, far above the forest. He knew that only a few small groves of stunted spruce and fir trees grow near mountain peaks. He carried bones and pieces of excess meat to the wolf. The wolf always ran away and hid when Nee Wahee approached and returned to the pile after the boy left.

Four coyotes watched from the surrounding trees. Whenever they came too close, Lonoch Moro growled and the smaller animals always ran away. Once a cougar watched from a nearby hill, but it never approached because of the white wolf.

Nee Wahee washed his hands in the stream whenever he

could safely leave the meat. His deerskin pants and jacket reeked from the smell of rotting meat. When he finally had enough jerky, Nee Wahee took off all of his clothes and washed them in the stream. He didn't want to smell like a wounded deer where there are cougars, bears and wolves.

He stuffed the purse full of jerky and put as much as he could in the bottom of the quiver. The jerky filled more than half the quiver and the arrows stuck out so far that Nee Wahee thought they might fall out when he climbed the jagged slopes that led to the mountain peaks. He slept naked in the blanket that night because his clothes were drying on a bush. The boy wrapped the blanket tightly around his body and dozed, waking frequently to search the surrounding trees and underbrush for animals, especially the white wolf.

The next morning Nee Wahee put on his clothes, extinguished the fire, and dragged the remainder of the deer's carcass deep into the forest. He threw the stakes and sticks from the rack into the woods. He erased all of his tracks by dragging a freshly cut fir branch over them. He searched throughout the campsite and removed all other evidence that he had been there. His father said that a person should respect the land and animals because they are part of the Soul of the World and everything is part of everything else. He bowed to the east where the sun was climbing into the early morning sky, chanted "tanake ahai supalo" seven times to his ancestors and raised his arms into the air toward the sun.

Lonoch Moro watched all of this from a distance and then trotted off to eat more of the deer's carcass. Nee Wahee heard him growl at an unseen intruder as he left the clearing and headed toward the high mountains.

High Mountains

Nee Wahee had no trail to follow as he climbed higher and higher through the trees and rocks toward the mountain peaks. Finally, he had climbed so high that most trees were left behind. Now there were grasses, bushes, a few late-blooming wildflowers, isolated small groves of trees and bare rock. Clouds drifted in and blocked his view of the mountain peaks. A rock rabbit scolded cheekily as he passed. Nee Wahee grinned at the rabbit and said, "You should be happy that my stomach is full Nahaho or you would be filling it."

As he climbed the air turned colder and wind buffeted him on ridges. He wrapped the blanket more tightly around his body and continued to climb. He thought: *Will I be able to climb to the top of the highest peak and wait there for a vision? How long should I wait? Could I freeze to death?*

Nee Wahee slipped on a narrow ledge along a precipice, but grabbed a jutting rock outcrop just before he fell over it. He crawled along the ledge until reaching a gentler slope, stood and continued the climb.

The boy looked up at the nearest tall peak which was now bathed in sunlight. He would sleep near that peak with hopes

of having a vision. He bent over and drank water that trickled from a melting snow bank. There was nothing but snow
and ice ahead and he climbed steadily on top the snow. At
times his feet broke through the hardened crust and he had
difficulty pulling out his legs. Sometimes he slipped and had
to catch himself before plummeting down a steep slope.

The boy stopped when he saw fresh wolf tracks in the
snow. He tightened his hand on the spear and looked all
around for the wolf, but didn't see it. Was it Lonoch Moro's
tracks or was another wolf interested in him? He sat on a
rock slab and continued watching for the wolf.

The mountain peak was just ahead and the boy climbed
a steep slope toward it. By this time it was evening and Nee
Wahee began searching for a place to sleep. Four huge rocks
had fallen in such a way that they made a cave large enough
for the boy. He pulled off his quiver, bow, and purse and put
them in a corner of the cave, leaving the spear and tomahawk
outside. Then, he removed small rocks from the cave's floor
and smoothed out the dirt to make a bed. He sat down to
face the valley and crossed his legs as the sky cleared.

Nee Wahee knew that his village was far away and on the
other side of the world. He thought about his father, mother
and sister Nee Roanee, or Little Raven. His mother would
worry and send prayers to the Great Spirit for his protection
and safe return; his father no doubt prayed that Nee Wahee
would have a great vision.

He took four pieces of jerky out of the quiver, but returned one knowing he might have many days and nights
ahead before he would be able to kill a deer or fish and he
knew that it was necessary to ration the food. He took small

bites, savoring the taste, and swallowed only after the meat was thoroughly chewed. He reached outside the shelter to grab handfuls of snow and let the snow melt in his hands before licking off the water.

The shrill cry of a wolf startled him. He grabbed his bow and took two arrows from the quiver and placed the toma-hawk nearer his right hand. His eyes searched the surrounding rocks, but he saw nothing in the fading daylight.

CONVERSATIONS WITH FOUR SPIRITS

An eagle glided over the peak as darkness of night swallowed the rugged landscape, its shrill scream piercing the night's tranquility. A cloud-shrouded half moon smiled down on the boy. Stars, seemingly more brilliant here than in the village, twinkled to tell him they were the souls of his ancestors. The brightest were souls of great leaders, the greatest of whom had wings and wandered among the other stars. Nee Wahee had much knowledge of the world and sky, thanks to teachings of his father and village elders. He remembered all that he had been taught and his head was full of memories as he dozed, sitting up with legs crossed and the blanket draped around his shoulders.

Mother Spirit (She Devil Mountain)

A sharp cold wind blew through mountain passes and swirled around Nee Wahee's small cave. He woke. The stars were even brighter than before. Dawn was probing the night's darkness and the boy could faintly see the rocks around him. One wandering star hugged the eastern horizon and he stared at it for a short time as it winked a friendly greeting and then disappeared.

Rustling sounds came from the high peak. He thought: *Is it the wolf or a giant bear making those noises?* Nee Wahee stood up, grabbed his tomahawk and spear, and prepared for battle.

A soft feminine voice whispered, "Nee Wahee, be not afraid."

Little bumps sprouted on his arms and his heart pumped so loud he could hear it. The unexpected voice was similar to his grandmother's. *Had she followed him into the mountains?*

"Nee Wahee, do not be afraid because I've been expecting you."

"Who are you, oh voice that whispers?"

"I am a spirit that will help with your quest. There is nothing to fear."

Nee Wahee looked closely at all rock outcrops around him and could see nothing that might be a spirit. He asked, "How did you get here and what are you doing on the mountain peak?"

"The Spirits of the Mountains have been here since long before the coming of humans to this world. Seven spirits live in these mountains. The Great Spirit of all Worlds closed the entrance to the Upper World to all of us because of our actions. We chose to follow the wrong spirit and were banished to these mountain peaks. Now, we exist between the Upper and Lower Worlds." She sighed before continuing. "Other spirits that were denied entrance to the Upper World are suffering in the Lower World where it is very hot and much wailing takes place, because they grieve about past wickedness. Spirits that helped beings of other worlds make their particular worlds better are in the Upper World where all is peaceful and where they experience only contentment and happiness. We spirits in these mountain peaks still have a chance to enter the Upper World if we find ways to make your world better for all living things."

The spirit paused as if out of breath and then said, "You will listen to six other spirits before returning to your village."

"I don't understand why the Spirits of the Mountains will talk to me."

"We'll tell many truths as guides as you plan for your future. Many omens have told us that you will be a great leader of your people during times of much sorrow and trouble. Your people will depend on strong leadership for survival and happiness. People from other parts of your region, strangers to you now, will be fed and protected by your people during times of famines and battles. They will become staunch allies and trusted friends. Everyone in your world must strive to become friends or they will not survive."

The sun peeked over the horizon and bathed the peak with bright light. The mother spirit sighed and whispered, "But most important to us, your successes or failures will determine our eternity."

"Are these spirits the feared devils or demons that hunters tell stories about?"

The mother spirit groaned and stillness settled over the mountains like smoke from a forest fire settles in deep canyons. Nothing except the wind was heard and Nee Wahee feared that she was angry. An eagle screamed at high pitch as it flew over the boy and landed near the peak.

After about a hundred heartbeats the spirit answered, "Some call us devils for we do them mischief, but our desire is to rise above that and to become spirits of the Upper World."

She paused again and Nee Wahee was tempted to speak, but didn't. He kicked a small red rock and it bounced down the slope. Finally she said, "Listen closely Nee Wahee, for the other spirits and I have advice that will make you into a great leader, a loved and respected leader who might someday, after your death, become one of the bright wanderers among the stars. You must remember all we say for our wisdom is vast and we understand and know both the past and the future."

"I'm ready to listen, Mother Spirit of the Mountains." A warm breeze caressed him. Nee Wahee looked toward the top of the peak and bowed his head because he was in the presence of something not of this world.

She said, "I speak to you of dreams and your heart."

"My dreams and my heart? I don't understand." Nee Wahee sat on the ground and crossed his legs.

The mother spirit whispered so low that the boy could barely hear. "Listen to your heart, because it knows every-thing. You can never keep your heart quiet and it will speak to you in the middle of the night and on the battlefield. It will tell you what to do, and you must always—always—listen to your heart."

"Are my dreams and my heart the same?" The boy watched geese fly over a deep canyon to the north, their honks rever-berating off sheer cliffs.

"Yes, you must follow your dreams because dreams become your heart. And dreams are the language of the Great Spirit.

He speaks to you through your dreams—and only you can understand his personal messages."

The mother spirit became quiet. A rock fell from a nearby cliff and hit rocks at the base, shattering the stillness. The eagle shrieked and rose from the peak to fly low over Nee Wahee's head.

She continued, "Wherever your heart is, that's where you find your treasure. But, wherever your treasure is, there also will be your heart. Take care of your heart, my son, because only through your heart will you find the important treasures in life."

"Are treasures the things I take from enemies and earn in battle?"

"No, Nee Wahee! No! No! True treasures are good friends, hard-won accomplishments, lifelong mates and your family members. Now, listen to this counsel very carefully and remember it." She raised her voice. "Love for your family is the major building block of happiness. Never forget that."

Another long silence followed. The mother spirit groaned again and several jagged boulders cascaded off the peak and hit the rocks below with resounding thumps, followed with noises made by sliding and bouncing fragments.

"I tire Nee Wahee. I have other tasks that need my attention. Tomorrow you will journey to the high peak that lies nearby. There you will talk to the Father Spirit of the Mountains. He has more to tell you. Remember his counsel."

The boy got up and bowed toward the mountain peak. He said, "Thank you, Mother Spirit of the Mountains." The wind strengthened and chilled Nee Wahee. He crawled back into the small cave made from leaning rocks and pulled the blanket tightly around him.

The white wolf appeared on a ridge above Nee Wahee, howled mournfully into the dawn, and walked closer. The boy grabbed his spear and began to rise, but the wolf whined and crawled toward Nee Wahee on its belly until the boy could have reached out and touched him. Nee Wahee put down the spear and Lonoch Moro curled up into a tight ball, his back against one of the leaning rocks. Nee Wahee had never seen a more beautiful animal in his entire life. The wolf whined softly, turned his head toward the boy and closed his eyes.

The boy tried to sleep, but his eyes would not remain closed and he kept repeating the advice given to him by the mother spirit in order to remember it. He would never forget her words. Finally, with chin resting on chest, the boy drifted into an uneasy sleep.

Father Spirit (He Devil Mountain)

A strong wind was blowing when Nee Wahee woke, bringing with it a thin covering of snow, some of which accumulated on the floor of the cave. A layer of gray clouds filtered the sun's rays and it was cold. Nee Wahee wanted to make a fire, but only a few dry twigs remained in his purse and no larger pieces of dry wood were lying nearby. He scooped snow into his hands and licked the water off the palms as it melted. He did this several times until he was no longer thirsty. The boy shivered as he took four pieces of jerky from the purse and chewed on them slowly, thinking about the other six spirits he would visit and the long hikes and climbs that would have to be made.

Lonoch Moro stirred, stood up, and shook the snow off his long coat of white hair. He looked at the boy. Nee Wahee threw the wolf two pieces of jerky. The wolf ate them and then stared expectantly at the boy.

"I'm sorry Lonoch Moro, but we must save as much of the jerky as possible because we have many spirits to meet." The white wolf raised his nose and trotted into the wind.

Clouds entombed the highest peak where the father spirit lived, but Nee Wahee remembered which way to go and walked toward it. The sun finally broke through the clouds and the peak seemed to dance in the radiance.

The sun was nearly overhead when Nee Wahee reached a narrow crevasse near the top of the peak where he huddled for protection from the cutting cold wind. He pulled the deerskin blanket over his shaking shoulders and stared at the peak. The sun was warm and he dozed.

The ground shook and rocks tumbled down steep slopes, some bouncing over high cliffs and exploding as they hit the rocks below. Nee Wahee woke. A fissure opened and hot steam sprayed into the air. Dark clouds smothered the sun.

A deep voice boomed from the top of the peak. "It's about time that you come to hear me." The deep voice trailed off into a whisper. "I have waited a long time." More rocks tumbled down the mountainside and the boy crouched deeper into the crevasse. Finally, the wind slowed and the sun peeked out from behind clouds.

Nee Wahee climbed out of the crevasse and stood with his arms opened toward the peak. "I'm Nee Wahee and am here to greet the father spirit and to hear his counsel."

Nothing happened for many heartbeats, but Nee Wahee

didn't care because he was warm standing in the sun's rays. He thought how nice it would be to have his mother cooking camas roots and chunks of venison for breakfast. He missed his family and knew that they worried about him. It seemed that he had been gone from home for most of his life.

On the ridge between peaks Lonoch Moro sat on his haunches and watched Nee Wahee, his gray and yellow eyes soft in the bright sunlight.

The ground trembled again and the deep resonating voice said, "I know who you are. I do not need to be reminded."

Several heartbeats passed before the father spirit asked, "What is it that you want to accomplish, Nee Wahee?"

"I don't know, Father Spirit of the Mountains."

"You must always know what you want. All people, even when very young, know their destiny and reason for being."

"Destiny? What is destiny?"

The voice boomed again and rocks rolled. "Destiny is what you've always wanted to accomplish; it is the ultimate goal that you want to reach during your lifetime."

"Will I be happy if I achieve my destiny?"

"Unfortunately, Nee Wahee, very few humans follow the path laid out for them which is the path to a fulfillment of destiny and subsequent happiness."

"I do not know my destiny."

"Oh—yes—you—do. And, you must remember that every person's obligation is to discover his or her destiny, and to carefully and faithfully follow the path that leads toward it."

The boy started to ask another question, but the booming voice stopped him. "Now go, Nee Wahee, and talk to spirits of the other mountains. They have more counsel for you. But just remember that you, and you alone, will be able to discover your destiny. And once you have discovered that destiny let nothing stand in your way of achieving it."

Nee Wahee sat down near the crevasse to wait for the spirit to speak again, but the rugged landscape remained quiet. The fissure closed with a grinding thump. He counted his heartbeats to three hundred as he waited. Finally, Nee Wahee stood and began walking toward the third peak. He tripped and slid across a sheet of ice on his buttocks before being stopped by a large rock. He got up, brushed off the ice and small pieces of rock and continued walking toward the third peak. Lonoch Moro trotted behind the boy.

Devious Spirit (Tower of Babel)

Nee Wahee walked past the mountain peak where he had spoken to the mother spirit. He heard soft humming and smiled, knowing that the she was happy. He waved and she acknowledged the wave by rolling a rock down the steepest slope toward a deep blue lake.

Afternoon sunlight wandered through the circular valley between two peaks and then departed, leaving long shadows behind. The boy finally stood at the base of a cliff near the third mountain peak. His legs ached from the long journey and it was necessary to rest them. He looked toward the very top of the peak. The mountain was not as high as the other two and its peak was long and jagged, looking much like the teeth of a wolverine. He didn't know what to expect and just stood there, waiting for something to happen. The sun was approaching the western horizon and Nee Wahee knew that it was time to find shelter for the night. He stared at the barren rock-strewn surface and saw nothing that would protect him while he slept. A few trees lined the slope below the jagged peak and Nee Wahee began walking toward them. He would have to sleep with his back against a tree trunk.

Dark clouds suddenly tumbled through and above the mountains and thunder bounced off cliffs and rolled along valley floors. Lightning crashed into the forest below; tree trunks split and shrieked in anguish as fire blazed from the wounds. The odor of charred wood permeated the air. Ducks flew above him in a tight pattern, their iridescent green heads shimmering as sunlight momentarily streaked through the ominous clouds.

A purring voice came from the jagged peak. "I can make a warm cave in this cliff where you can rest tonight."

Nee Wahee looked toward the peak. "That would be nice, oh Spirit of the Mountains. Thank you."

"But I won't young man because you have to suffer more."

Nee Wahee frowned and asked, "Are you a bad spirit who will harm me?"

The jagged peak chuckled. "No, I won't harm you. You have heard advice from the father and mother spirits, but my advice to you is to get off my mountain if you fear suffering."

More thunder rolled across the sky and the boy, now afraid for his life, turned to leave.

The voice rasped, "Stay and listen. Remember Nee Wahee, that the fear of suffering is worse than suffering itself." A boulder fell from the cliff and bounced down the slope toward

Nee Wahee and the boy moved quickly out of its way.

The spirit chuckled and said, "I'll put up with this discussion because I want to spend eternity in the Upper World. Unfortunately, I have to coddle you to do that."

"I can get along without you."

The voice deepened. "No you can't. You must listen to the counsel of all mountain spirits. And, you must remember every word. Your people will someday need our counsel for their survival because you, Nee Wahee, will lead them along trails where every step is dangerous."

"Can I not trust someone else to lead?"

The spirit sighed as if tired of the conversation. "You must trust everyone at least once. Never lose faith in your fellow humans, but trust no other person to lead your people. You alone must lead. Otherwise, enemies will kill the people of your village. Everyone will vanish from this world. You and your people will no longer exist."

Lightning struck at the base of the cliff and Nee Wahee jumped back in fear. He stumbled over a rock and fell, and then jumped up to look at the mountain again. Blood flowed from a wound on his wrist.

He yelled, "I already have enemies. Some of the warriors in my village are jealous that I am the son of a chief. They want me to die." Nee Wahee felt very sad after he spoke those words and looked away from the peak and into the valley below. He didn't want the spirit to see his tear-filled eyes.

"Oh Nee Wahee, little boy trying to be a man, your worst enemy can become a best friend. Learn to know a man's desires and what and how he thinks. You must know what is inside a man's house because you can trust no man, even once, if you do not know what's in his house."

"What is a man's house?"

"A man's house is what he thinks, what he wants, and the moral fiber of his friends and family members. A man associates with people as much like him as possible. Bad friends and bad family members form a bad man; good friends and good family members make a good man. If you are ever in doubt, remember that a good man generally has a good mother. Meet his mother and you meet the man when he was a boy."

Tears welled up in Nee Wahee's eyes again as he thought of his own mother and his heart filled with love for her. She was good to everyone and never criticized or gossiped.

The boy stared at a dark cloud that scooted across the sky. "How do I know, spirit, that I can trust myself?"

The spirit laughed and the sound echoed off surrounding cliffs. "First, learn to keep all of your promises. Remember that when you give a promise it becomes who you are. A promise is an agreement that cannot be ignored. By keeping all promises you will learn to trust yourself. That is a large part of what is called *integrity*."

The setting sun peeked out from behind a black cloud, casting a purplish-pink glow over the cliff. The boy looked along the base of the cliff and saw a shadow that wasn't there before. It was the opening to a cave. He looked at the peak and said, "Thank you for the cave, oh Spirit of the Mountains."

The spirit's voice softened. "Rest well Nee Wahee, for you will be journeying long distances for conversations with four other spirits. You must listen closely to what they say because their counsel will make your life worthwhile and you'll be able to achieve your destiny. Only then will you be truly happy. I wish you the good favor of our Great Spirit as you journey through life."

A light rain began falling as the boy made his way to the cave. He ducked inside. Someone, or something, had piled branches on the floor of the cave and Nee Wahee started a fire with dry twigs and pieces of flint from his purse. A spring dripped water onto the floor of the cave and the boy made a small basin in the mud to catch the water. After drinking his fill Nee Wahee ate four pieces of jerky, pulled the blanket over his shoulders and sat on the rocky floor of the cave. Lonoch Moro entered the cave and drank water from the small basin. He looked at Nee Wahee expectantly, curled himself into a ball near the fire, and rested his head on outstretched paws. Branches crackled in the fire and flames cast shadows on the walls of the cave. Nee Wahee's mind swam in tight circles as he remembered all that the three spirits had told him.

Melancholy Spirit (Mt. Ogre)

It rained hard during the night. Nee Wahee stayed under the blanket as long as he could. Even though the rain had stopped the air was still heavy with moisture. He glanced at the spot where Lonoch Moro had slept, but the wolf was gone. He rekindled the fire and sat next to it as he ate three pieces of jerky and a few berries he found beneath the hooks and line at the bottom of his purse. He looked at the wound on his wrist. It was healing. The boy stood up, turned to the fire pit, and extinguished the remaining coals with his foot. He broke several dry twigs into small pieces to be used later for kindling and put them inside his purse.

Nee Wahee picked up the weapons, walked boldly through the cave's opening, carefully picked a path along a steep slope where rocks had fallen from the cliff and hiked south and over the next ridge. He saw another high mountain peak and headed toward it at a fast walk.

The boy walked across several large footprints of a bear. He stopped and looked closely at them. They had been made since the rain. He thought: *Is the bear stalking me?* He took off his quiver, counted the arrows and tested the tautness of the bowstring. He would be ready if the bear attacked.

It was a relatively easy climb to the top of the rather flat peak. He sat on a boulder and watched as shadows shortened with the rising sun. Soon, the sun would be directly overhead. Nee Wahee stretched out on the boulder and dozed.

A voice woke him. "The other spirits said that you would come to my mountain today. I have more counsel for you." A sigh echoed back and forth across a valley below the boy.

Nee Wahee sat upright and rubbed his eyes. He looked all around. The rocks were coated with drops of water even though the sun was now overhead.

"I'm here to listen to your wisdom, oh Spirit of the Mountains."

"That's good. But, I'm melancholy because I'm tired of having been part of this mountain for such a long time. I've been trapped, seemingly forever, between the Lower and Upper Worlds." Water dripped off the cliffs like giant teardrops.

"I hope that I can be of help to all of the spirits."

"Help will be given only if you heed our words and make

your world a better place for humans and for all other crea-
tures. It is only then that we'll enter the Upper World."

Quiet descended over the mountain and nearby valleys.
Two red-tailed hawks glided above the peak, looking for
something to eat. The cliffs stopped weeping and moisture on
the rocks dried. Nee Wahee took off his deerskin jacket and
laid it next to him on a boulder. One of the hawks screamed
as it flew above him. Ants followed an unmarked trail across
the boulder near his feet, their little antennae moving rapidly
as they talked over the day's tasks. Nee Wahee scanned the
landscape for the bear, but did not see it. A large eagle, probably the same one he had seen before, circled high above the
hawks.

The spirit sighed. Pent-up sadness dripped from his voice
as he talked. "You must remember, Nee Wahee, that all things
are one. Everything on earth is continuously transformed because the earth is alive and has a soul."

Nee Wahee frowned, but the spirit continued his counsel.
"Yes, everything has a soul just like you, whether it is veg-
etable, mineral, or animal—or even just a simple thought."

"What is a soul?"

The spirit hesitated for several heartbeats and then said,
"It is the spiritual principle embodied in the universe, particularly in humans, but also in all things created by the Great
Spirit, the giver of life to everything in your world and in all
worlds."

"I think I understand."

"You won't understand until you reach an old age."

Another sigh escaped the mountain. "You must know,
Nee Wahee, that we'll be watching throughout your life.

When you are in such peril that death or injury is certain, we'll help without your knowledge."

"I thank you for the promise, but hope that I'll never need your help."

The spirit's voice strengthened. "Nee Wahee, you can change the world. You have the strength and intelligence to be a wise chief. Don't let insignificant things keep you from your destiny. Now be off. Go talk to the other spirits."

Nee Wahee picked up his weapons and other gear and began walking toward the next mountain peak.

EL VIEJO RESTS

El Viejo's head droops lower and lower as he fights to stay awake. He stops talking and I look up. The fire has burned down to glowing embers. His eyes close and shoulders droop forward, bringing his head near the embers. I clear my throat and the old man's glazed eyes stare at me with no apparent recognition. Finally, his eyes focus.

"I'm tired and must sleep. If you want, I'll continue the story tomorrow when the sun is bright."

"Do you have anything to sleep in besides the blanket?"

"No my son. I'll be fine. I've slept many nights like this."

I fall asleep and when I wake the sun has not yet climbed over the Seven Devils Mountains. El Viejo is still asleep. He had slumped over during the night with feet drawn under his small body. I cover him with my sleeping bag and walk into the trees to collect more dry wood, carry back an armload, and stir the fire to wake it. I put dry twigs on the embers and blow on them. They burst into flame and I slowly feed the fire larger and larger sticks of wood. I walk to the creek and dip water into a pot and put it on the two flat rocks within the fire ring. I dump in coffee grounds as the water boils.

El Viejo raises his head and looks around the small campsite as if he hasn't seen it before. He whispers, "The smell of
coffee woke me." In the light of dawn his face seems even
more wrinkled and shrunken than it had the night before.
He looks more like a mummy than a living person. I stand,
pour coffee into a cup and give it to him over the fire. He
grabs the hot cup and holds it tightly in his gnarled hands,
letting the steam rise into narrow nostrils.

He raises white eyebrows. "Thank you mi amigo—my
friend." He lifts the cup, as if in a toast, and looks into my
eyes.

I avert my eyes, drink directly from the pot and dump the
wet coffee grounds into the fire. I pour water from a canteen
into the pot and put in three packets of instant oats as the
water heats. Soon it is bubbling. I stir for several seconds and
take the pot off the fire. I dump more than half the porridge
into a blue plastic bowl, shake in some raisins and put in four
spoons of dried milk. After stirring for a few seconds I hand
the bowl to El Viejo. He shovels the food into his mouth
as though starved. I spoon the remaining porridge into his
bowl and he also eats that.

He apologizes. "I have much hunger this morning."

I eat some raisins from the plastic bag and give the bag to
El Viejo. He grabs a handful and munches on them with his
gums. Brown spittle dribbles down his chin. He unties the
pink bandana from around his neck, wipes spittle from his
chin and mouth and reties the bandana.

By now it's nine o'clock and rays of sunlight are filtering
through the trees. I put more wood on the fire. El Viejo remains huddled under the sleeping bag. He reaches out, grabs

his purse, takes out the pipe and fills it with tobacco. I hand him a burning twig and he lights the pipe, sucking the smoke in hungrily. He slides over to a large rock, dragging the sleeping bag with him, and rests his back against the granite. His eyes close. I wash the pot and utensils in the creek and return to the fire. I put moleskin on my feet and pull on socks and boots. I look through my large backpack to make sure I have enough food for three more days of work. I count four cans of tuna, two cans of mushroom soup, three small cans of sliced peaches, six packets of instant oatmeal, five packets of hot chocolate, a quarter-pound or so of coffee, two packages of freeze-dried beef stew, and a pound of dry macaroni.

El Viejo throws the sleeping bag to me and I roll and tie it into a compact bundle. I put it in a black garbage bag for protection from rain and toss it on the ground. I take the fishing gear apart and put it inside the backpack along with the pot and eating utensils. I toss two canteens of water, a can of tuna and a bag of peanuts and raisins into the small daypack for my lunch.

The old man is watching through half-closed eyes. They snap open and I stare into their bottomless black pupils. I expect the eyes to speak, but it is El Viejo's mouth that moves. "Thank you for your food and fire. I should be going now. I know you have much work to do."

"Please—don't go. You haven't finished the story about the boy and the seven spirits. I have two or three more days of work and then I'll drive to Riggins for more supplies. I have plenty of food left until then." I pick up the map case, open it and stare at the area I need to study during the time I have left on this trip. I say, "I have room in my truck if you'd like to go to Riggins. In fact, I can take you to either Lewiston or Boise."

"No thank you. I have a way out."

I stare at him and ask, "How is that?"

"The same way I came in. Don't worry."

I shake my head. "You are a strange man, Viejo. Please continue the story. It's important that I hear all of it. I can postpone my work a day. I'll just go to town a day later than I had planned and eat more fish for my meals if I run out of other food."

El Viejo chuckles and asks, "Where did I stop?"

"The boy was hiking to another peak to hear advice from a fifth spirit."

"Ah, yes." El Viejo fills his pipe with tobacco and lights it with a burning twig. "During the next part of his quest Nee Wahee was nearly killed." He looks closely at me and once again stares into my eyes. "If he had been killed, you and I would not be having this conversation."

I want to ask what he means, but instead I plead, "Please Viejo, continue the story."

The old man leans back on the rock, pulls the blanket around his legs and tells the rest of the story.

THE VISION QUEST CONTINUES

It was past mid-day and Nee Wahee hiked south toward the next peak. It seemed far and his feet became sore because he was walking on sharp rocks of many sizes and the soles of his moccasins had worn thin. The boy stopped to rest in a meadow near a spring that trickled from a small pile of rocks. He took two pieces of jerky from his purse and chewed on them. Stooping over, he filled both palms with water, raised them to his lips and drank.

Loud noises made by sliding and tumbling rocks alerted Nee Wahee that something big was coming toward him. He looked back along the trail he had made while crossing a talus slope. The largest brown bear Nee Wahee had ever seen was sniffing Nee Wahee's tracks. The bear had a hump on its shoulders. It was a member of the most feared family of great bears, bears that had killed many of the boy's people.

The boy thought: *Why hasn't the bear gone to sleep for the winter?* He answered his own question. *It's too early and the bear is still hungry.*

The giant bear raised its nose and looked at the boy.

Nee Wahee knew that bears have poor eyesight and he crouched down to blend in with the rocks. He didn't move. The breeze was blowing from the boy toward the bear, however, and Nee Wahee could see that the bear smelled him.

The bear ran toward Nee Wahee with a gait that eats up distances much faster than a boy can run. Nee Wahee looked around for a steep rock to climb because there were no trees. A nearby rock was high and steep. Nee Wahee grabbed his weapons and climbed the rock. It was a tough climb and he was nearly out of breath when he reached the top. The bear arrived in the meadow, stood against the rock and stared at Nee Wahee.

The beast roared and Nee Wahee looked down into its huge mouth. One canine tooth was missing from the top of its jaw and the smell of the bear's breath gagged the boy. The bear swiped at Nee Wahee and its claws nearly hit the boy's feet.

The bear tried to climb the steep rock face, but slipped and fell backwards. Another roar came from the bear. It turned and scrambled up a slope near the rock. Suddenly, it was above the boy. The angry and hungry bear stood on its hind legs and roared again. Saliva dripped from its mouth and wet the rocks below.

Nee Wahee calmly picked up his bow. He stood on top the rock and fit an arrow onto the bowstring. He knew it would take much more than one arrow to kill the beast, so he put another arrow at his feet where it would be easy to reach. The bear walked toward the boy on its hind legs, roaring and opening its cavernous mouth. The boy pulled back on the bowstring, ready to send an arrow into the bear's heart.

Nee Wahee glimpsed a white blur as Lonoch Moro hurtled past him and landed on the bear's chest. The bear fell backwards under the white wolf's weight and the two animals rolled and slid down the slope biting, growling and roaring.

Finally, the animals stopped rolling and sliding and stood eye to eye. The bear roared and the white wolf growled. Blood ran from the bear's neck and from the wolf's right shoulder where long bloody grooves had been made by the bear's claws.

The bear hit Lonoch Moro with a paw. The wolf flew through the air and landed on the ground near Nee Wahee. Blood now flowed from Lonoch Moro's other shoulder, which had deep grooves cut into it from the bear's claws. The wolf was only able to rise part way and remained there with his head down as if waiting for the fatal blow. The bear shuffled toward the wolf and boy on its hind legs.

Nee Wahee turned his bow toward the bear and released the carefully aimed arrow. It flew straight and hit the bear in the chest. The bear roared and looked at the boy, who was still standing on the rock. Blood spurted out from along the arrow's shaft and stained the ground around the combatants. Nee Wahee fit a second arrow onto the bowstring just as Lonoch Moro leaped again, grabbed the bear's throat and wrestled it to the ground. The bear stood, hit Lonoch Moro a second time and sent the wolf flying through the air to land in an unmoving heap. The bear walked toward the wolf and Nee Wahee shot another arrow; this one penetrated its ribcage behind the left foreleg.

The bear stopped and pawed at both arrows. Nee Wahee jumped off the rock and ran toward the bear with spear raised in his right hand. He carried the obsidian knife in his other hand. The boy shouted as loudly as he could while running toward the confused and wounded bear.

Nee Wahee was within a few strides of the bear when it turned away and ran down the slope. The boy followed the bear. It stopped and turned toward the boy as if to attack, but another loud shout confused it even more. The beast turned and loped slowly toward a grove of spruce trees.

The still-frightened boy returned to help Lonoch Moro,

looking over his shoulder toward the grove of trees after every step. The wolf sat up as the boy approached. Nee Wahee treated the wounds by washing them with water from the spring. The grateful wolf licked the boy's hands while its wounds were being washed.

Conversations
With Three More Spirits

The wolf and Nee Wahee rested for several hundred heartbeats and watched the slope below them for signs of the bear's return. Nothing stirred. The boy picked up his weapons, quiver, purse, and deerskin blanket and walked on toward the next peak. The wolf limped along behind the boy, stopping often to lick the deep shoulder wounds.

An eagle flew low over them and the wolf raised his head and yelped in apparent recognition. It looked like the same eagle that had flown over them before.

Pessimistic Spirit (Mt. Goblin)

Nee Wahee and Lonoch Moro reached the next peak and sat down in its shadow. The boy checked Lonoch Moro's wounds as the wolf licked the boy's hands and face. Finally, they stretched out on the rocky slope and dozed.

A bright light burst from the peak and a shrill voice screamed, "You have taken too much time getting here, lazy boy. I've been waiting all day. No—I've been waiting forever.

Come here at once!"

Lonoch Moro whined and remained lying on the ground, but Nee Wahee grasped his weapons and scampered up the steep slope that led to the peak. He arrived nearly out of breath and said, "Don't be angry with me, oh Spirit of the Mountains. Please don't be angry."

The spirit's voice came from a narrow gorge near the peak's highest point. "We have many things to discuss and you dawdle like a little child. You spend time playing with a bear and a wolf when you should be listening to the Spirits of the Mountains. You'll never be a warrior and a leader if you act like this. I should throw you off the mountain. And I can do it my young guest. Believe me, I can do it."

A loud grunt escaped from the gorge before the voice continued speaking. "Anyway, I don't think you can help us and I've told the other spirits my thoughts. How can we trust a little boy with our eternity? Such thoughts sadden me." A rock tumbled down the mountain's slope and the spirit's voice grew softer until it was only a whisper. "We are not wise to put our trust in someone who is afraid of the dark."

"I am no longer afraid of the dark. You can trust me. I won't disappoint the Spirits of the Mountains."

The spirit groaned and muttered, "Harump! I've heard such promises before. Few humans keep promises."

A rock rolled from the peak as if something were sitting there. Nee Wahee shaded his eyes, but could see nothing.

"It will not help to shade your eyes, Nee Wahee. You cannot see me." Several hundred heartbeats later the spirit spoke again. "I have some counsel I must give you. Listen closely."

Nee Wahee was nodding, fighting hard to stay awake, and his head dropped down.

"Wake up boy! Are you listening?"

Nee Wahee shook his head to clear it. "I'm listening, spirit."

"Nee Wahee, you must always remember that when you want something, and want it with all of your heart, the entire universe helps you achieve it."

"The entire universe?"

"Yes, every human plays a central role in the history of the world. The Great Spirit has prepared a path for everyone to follow. Everyone has a destiny, but I'm discouraged because few humans find it."

"I can't believe I'm important to the history of the world!"

"Believe it my son, and also know this. It is the responsibility of all humans to nourish the world, and this world will become either better or worse depending on whether humans become better or worse. Humans must endeavor to be in harmony with each other and with all other living things."

Silence again fell over the mountain and a sharp wind blew between the peaks. Nee Wahee tightened the blanket as he waited for the spirit to tell him more. In the distance a bull elk brayed to attract a mate. A small rock rolled down the slope near the boy.

The shrill voice pierced the air, this time much louder than before. "I'm tired of you. Now get off my mountain! Get off my mountain!"

Nee Wahee stumbled from the peak and down the mountainside with tears in his eyes. *Why,* he thought, *does the spirit have to be mean?*

He looked for a place to make camp, but there was no cave or even sharp ridge to break the force of the wind. He walked down a long rugged slope and finally reached a small lake. Three large round rocks were bunched close together and he wedged his body among them. He rested while his breathing slowed. The ground was wet and odors of moss and lichens permeated the small space.

A nighthawk swooped over the lake, moaning for lost souls of its companions. A fish jumped from the water and fell back with a resounding splash.

Lonoch Moro slowly picked his way down the slope after Nee Wahee. He had licked all blood from his shoulders and ribs and the wounds were clean and beginning to heal. The wolf drank water from the lake and walked over to Nee Wahee after its thirst was quenched. He stuck out his nose and Nee Wahee petted the animal's head. The wolf curled up to lie down near the boy.

"Lonoch Moro, you saved my life. Thank you." The wolf licked the boy's hand and laid his head on outstretched paws.

Nee Wahee was hungry, but his purse and quiver contained only a few more pieces of jerky. He thought about the fish that had jumped from the water and decided to catch that fish, or one of its companions. From the purse he took out a long piece of line and a hook. He selected a flexible tree branch and cut off the small branches and twigs with his tomahawk. He attached the hook to the line and the line to the end of the branch.

He turned over a green moss-covered rock and found several worms squirming in the moist soil. He fastened one to the hook and crawled slowly and silently to the lake's edge. He cast the bait far out and slowly hauled in the line. He felt a tug on the line and jerked it. The fish was caught. It was of medium size and Nee Wahee cut off the head and gutted and skinned the fish with his teeth and knife. He threw the entrails, skin and head to the wolf and ate the remaining meat raw. The meat felt good in his stomach. Lonoch Moro whined for more.

"You cannot have the bones Lonoch Moro because they could injure your stomach." Nee Wahee threw the bones far out into lake. The wolf whined again and the boy said, "Okay my valued friend, I'll catch another fish for us. I can also eat more."

The boy put another worm on the hook and caught a second fish. This one was larger and he gave the wolf most of it after taking out the bones. Lonoch Moro ate the fish and looked expectantly at Nee Wahee for more.

The boy shook his head and said, "I'm very sorry Lonoch Moro, but there is no more to eat and we must sleep." The boy looked up at a twinkling wanderer that had just arrived in the darkening sky and yelled, "Ee-yah. Thank you Great Spirit for providing us food."

By then night had fallen. Nee Wahee put the weapons close by and tucked the blanket around his body. He thought about the advice that had been given to him by the mountain spirits. He repeated the spirits' words over and over to remember them.

Rocks tumbled down the slope of a mountain and Nee

Wahee thought about the bear. He checked the weapons. A raven called out in the far distance. Its mate answered. Odors of spruce trees and wet moss drifted through the boy's nostrils. He had missed those smells when he was high in the mountains. The boy gazed at the stars, particularly at a large wanderer that hung in the southern sky. He curled up inside the blanket and slipped into a deep sleep with the white wolf lying by his side.

Shy Spirit (Mt. Belial)

A dense fog greeted Nee Wahee when he woke. It was so thick that he could see only the ground in front of his feet. Frost draped over the weapons, quiver and purse. He shivered in the cold, ate three pieces of jerky and drank water from the lake. He looked for Lonoch Moro, but the wolf had left sometime during the night. Above the fog an eagle screamed. A wolf, probably Lonoch Moro, answered the eagle with a series of yaps and a long mournful howl. The boy returned to the shelter and sat under the blanket until the fog began lifting. A twig snapped in a nearby grove of fir trees and Nee Wahee grabbed his spear, thinking that it might be the bear. He listened for a time equal to at least a thousand heartbeats, but heard nothing more. By then the fog had dispersed and the boy stood, picked up his weapons, purse and quiver, threw the deerskin blanket over his shoulder and headed toward the next mountain.

This mountain peak was not as high as the others and he reached it after warmth from the sun had made the morning dampness disappear. He sat on a flat purple rock to wait for the mountain spirit to speak.

He became bored with waiting and got up to leave for the next mountain, but a faint rustling noise came from a jagged rock near the peak and a warm breeze enveloped him. He looked toward the peak and said, "Speak to me, oh Spirit of the Mountains."

More rustling noises came from the jagged rock. Finally, a very soft voice said, "My advice is not important for finding and achieving your destiny."

"The advice and counsel I received from the other mountain spirits are important. Please give me yours."

The shy spirit whispered, "My best advice has to do with a life that is worth living."

"I can barely hear you. Please speak louder."

The spirit repeated his words, but this time louder. "My best advice has to do with a life that is worth living. Learn the language of enthusiasm, of things accomplished with love and purpose and as part of a search for something desired."

"I am enthusiastic. I have a great future and will be helping my people. But, I'm afraid of the unknown."

The spirit coughed before speaking again. "Humans need not fear the unknown if they are capable of achieving what they need and want. I think you are capable, otherwise I wouldn't waste time on you."

The spirit hesitated for several heartbeats and then said, "Now go to the next mountain and heed our final counsel."

"I think you have more to tell me."

"How do you know that?" The spirit's voice was gruff.

"Because you have not told me enough and I really understand only part of what you've told me."

"I'm sorry," said the spirit, "I do have other things to tell you, but I'm already tired of talking to you."

Nee Wahee said, "Tell me more, spirit. Please tell me more."

A soft sigh came from the spirit. "Well, Nee Wahee, I've been thinking that you're becoming a man too soon. You should do child things when you're a child and man things when you're a man. When you return to your village be sure to play with friends, swim in lakes and streams, hunt for rabbits and roll rocks off mountains to watch them tumble into valleys far below. Run until you are weary and can run no more. Race the deer and elk. Be a strong boy and you will be a strong man."

"I'm ready now to be a man and a brave warrior."

The spirit whispered, "That will happen too soon, my boy. It will happen too soon."

The spirit wasn't through. "And, when you become leader of the village make sure that children act like children until they have to become men and women."

"Thank you Spirit of the Mountains. I'll remember your wisdom and advice."

As the boy walked down the slope of the mountain he heard the spirit say, "Live your life well Nee Wahee so that we Spirits of the Mountains can journey to the Upper World and live there for all eternity."

Nee Wahee waved to the mountain peak and began walking toward the last of the seven mountains, which was only a short distance away.

By now the boy's legs were as strong as large branches of a willow tree and his lungs no longer labored for air. He smiled and thought: *I have conquered the mountains and will never*

*again be afraid of the dark and of things not understood. As I
grow older I'll try to understand all things in my world and then
I'll teach my knowledge to others.*

Teacher Spirit (Devils Throne)

Nee Wahee walked along a ridge toward the mountain
where he would talk to the seventh and last spirit. Lonoch
Moro joined him and the boy could see that the wolf's
wounds were healing well. Nee Wahee was excited because
he knew this spirit would say things so important that, by
the time he left the mountains to return home, he would
understand his destiny.

He looked over his shoulder often to see if the bear was
following. Had he killed the bear? Nee Wahee felt sad as he
remembered the bear running away with arrows protruding
from its chest and ribs. The bear had been doing only what
it had to do in order to live. Nee Wahee's flesh would have
put more meat on the bear to help it survive the long winter.
Now, the great animal would need the long winter to heal its
wounds.

The ridge ended at a steep cliff. A large rock jutted out
from the top of the cliff and Nee Wahee sat down on it.
From where he sat the boy looked directly at the peak. A
breeze crept under the blanket and massaged him with cold
fingers. He shivered and tightened the blanket around his
shaking body.

Nee Wahee glanced at his feet and smiled because both
big toes had worn holes in the tops of his moccasins. He
raised his hands and looked at them; they were no longer
the hands and fingers of a boy, but of a young man. He felt

tightness across his shoulders and realized that he had grown much stronger during his long journey.

Lonoch Moro sat on his haunches and looked at the boy with wonderment and longing in his eyes. But then the wolf turned his head, stared at the mountain peak and whined. Nee Wahee stroked the head and ears of the big wolf and softly called his name. He put his head on the wolf's neck, closed his eyes and welcomed the first few breaths of sleep.

A deep and friendly voice came from the mountain peak. "Do not sleep Nee Wahee for I have things to tell you."

Nee Wahee said, "I've come a long way to hear you, oh Spirit of the Mountains."

"We spirits have great hopes that your journey will not have been in vain."

Nee Wahee waited for the spirit to say more, but the peak remained quiet. Finally the boy asked, "Are you a spirit only in this world?"

A rumble came from deep under the mountain and the ground shook. Nee Wahee was afraid and turned away from his perch to run away.

"Don't run, Nee Wahee. I don't know how to tell you that I've been to other worlds and talked to beings something like you. They were not shaped like you, but had great intelligence. I taught them many things about their lives and worlds. Everyone and everything needs help to find and fulfill their destinies."

"You have lived a long time?"

"Since before your world formed from the cosmos."

Nee Wahee said, "I do not understand the word cosmos."

"Cosmos is both the substance and the order of the universe. Your world is a small but important part of that order, as are you."

"I am part of the cosmos?"

"Yes, you are part of the cosmos."

"Spirit, do you have a name?"

The spirit started to speak, but hesitated. The boy looked up at the peak that towered above him. For the first time, he was able to see the eyes of a spirit. The eyes were as black as charcoal left behind after a fire. Nee Wahee stared into them and was drawn into deep pools of still water.

The spirit spoke, "I have been called many names, but you will remember me as Kowamano, or Great Eagle. However, my name is not important."

The boy looked more closely at the mountain peak as clouds surrounded it. The prominence in front of the peak and the eyes formed the head of an eagle.

Nee Wahee stammered as he asked, "Do you have counsel to give me, Kowamano?"

"You already have received most of the advice you need. But, I do have three important things to say that must always be remembered."

"Go ahead and tell me."

The spirit said, "First, you must understand that simple things in life are the most extraordinary. The fragrance of a flower and the flutter of a butterfly's wings are simple, yet they are also part of the cosmos. Stop often to listen, to smell, to feel, to taste and to see. Drink in the simple things of life at every opportunity."

"Thank you. I understand and shall remember."

"The second thing is this. Live your life to the fullest. If you can concentrate mostly on the present you'll be a happy man. Live as though there is no afterlife. Your life should be a party, a grand festival, because life is the moment you are living right now."

No more words came from the mountain peak. Nee Wahee waited patiently. The clouds that had partly enveloped the peak floated off to the north.

Finally the boy asked, "Do you have one more thing to tell me, Spirit Kowamano?"

"I have one more point to make, after which you must leave. It is this. Love a woman without owning her, because when a man truly loves a woman he always strives to become a better person. Remember that you can never own another person like you own a dog."

The spirit whispered, "You have heard all that we spirits have to tell. Now, go back to your village."

Nee Wahee gathered his weapons, threw the blanket over his shoulder and started to leave. He turned toward the peak and asked, "Will I ever meet you or the other spirits again?"

The spirit answered, "We spirits will help you during both this life and your next life." Kowamano's voice deepened and the whole mountain shook as he said, "And yes, Nee Wahee, we will meet again but not during this lifetime."

NEE WAHEE GOES HOME

Nee Wahee walked away from the peak and down the side of the mountain. He had experienced the vision that he needed to become a warrior and perhaps later on, chief of his village. Now he would go home to tell his vision to the village elders. He sat against a rock and ate the remaining jerky, all the while remembering everything the spirits had said. He spoke to the emptiness of the mountains, repeating out loud all the advice and counsel the seven spirits had given him. He would leave almost nothing out when the elders asked him to tell them about his vision. He could not tell them about Lonoch Moro because he knew that some of the warriors would hunt and kill the wolf.

Nee Wahee slept that night at the edge of the forest near a stream. He rested on a long flat rock and nestled under the blanket. Lonoch Moro curled up beside him and licked Nee Wahee's hands and face. The wolf's long hair warmed the boy. Nee Wahee slept and voices of the spirits ran through his mind as he dreamed. The next morning he took out a hook and line, attached them to a tree branch, and caught three small trout. He ate two fish raw and gave the largest

fish, plus the remains of the other two fish, to the wolf. The
boy hiked down the mountain to a valley where he encountered a game trail. He walked north along trails and streams
toward his village.

He caught more fish to eat as he journeyed toward home.
The berries were gone because it also had grown cold in the
valleys. After four days of steady walking, and some running,
he was back on a familiar trail leading to the village.

Lonoch Moro had remained with Nee Wahee during the
trip back to the village, but when they arrived at the massive
rock near the trail, he licked Nee Wahee's hand, whined and
trotted back the way they had come. The boy called to him
and the wolf stopped, stared at Nee Wahee for many heartbeats, and then turned and disappeared into the forest.

Nee Wahee climbed the massive rock and put his weapons and quiver in the same hole where they had been hidden
before. He covered them with small rocks and soil and
marked the spot with a rock cairn. He leaped back onto the
trail and began running toward the village.

Nee Wahee called out to his mother as he approached the
village. His mother and Nee Roanee embraced him. They
walked past the council lodge where his father sat near the
entrance, smoking a long-stemmed pipe. The chief didn't
look at them. His mother prepared a meal of boiled Camas
tubers, venison, and flat bread made from dried tubers of the
balsamroot plant. She stared at Nee Wahee as the boy ate, her
eyes moving slowly over his body.

"You've grown much since you left, my son. You're tall
and muscles tug at what is left of the clothes I made. You're
nearly a man. I'm happy to have you safe at home."

Nee Roanee scooted over to sit close to Nee Wahee. Her small fingers stroked his neck and face. She said, "Please tell us about your vision. I know it was a good one."

"I can only tell the elders, but I'll tell you and mother after I talk to them."

Nee Wahee finished eating and climbed into his bed for a short nap. However, he slept the whole night without waking, even though his father came into the lodge, ate dinner and talked in hushed tones with his wife and daughter.

Village Elders Ask Questions

Dawn crept into the village on silent wings and the chief left the family lodge before Nee Wahee woke. His mother shook the boy and told him to hurry to the council lodge because the elders were waiting. The boy rose from his bed, put on clean clothes his mother set out for him and stumbled to the fire where boiled camas tubers and strips of dried venison were sitting on a reed mat. He ate the food hurriedly and bounded out the door.

Nee Wahee entered the council lodge and stood outside the ring of seated elders facing Hoa Nakoa, the senior member of the council. The elders asked many questions and the boy stood in place as he answered them. The elders stopped often to pass a long-stemmed pipe around the circle of men and each took a deep draw from the pipe before passing it on. His father sat quietly on the fringe of the circle as Nee Wahee told them about the journey and about the seven spirits and their advice and counsel. He remembered everything that had happened and every word spoken by the spirits. He told them about his battle with the humped bear, but he didn't tell them about the great white wolf. The elders and Nee Wahee only took breaks to eat and sleep. They questioned the boy for most of two days and they asked him to repeat the advice and counsel the spirits had given him. This time through the story, however, no one interrupted Nee Wahee. The elders were gravely quiet and Nee Wahee was afraid their silence meant that they didn't believe him. They never asked how he acquired the weapons. At mid-afternoon on the second day Hoa Nakao told him to leave the lodge and to come back when the sun had set behind the western horizon.

Nee Wahee wandered around the village. He whittled a whistle from a small branch of mountain mahogany and taught Nee Roanee to make sounds with it. The sun seemed to stop in its journey across the western sky while he waited.

Kano Capoee ran from his parent's lodge to greet Nee Wahee. Kano Capoee had also become taller and stronger. The two boys held their right arms together to feel the blood beat in the other's veins and then embraced.

Kano Capoee told Nee Wahee about his vision because he had already talked to the elders. After Kano Capoee left the village for his vision he had walked north to a large river. He sat on its bank near a wide bend for six suns. He ate no food and only drank water from the river. On the seventh morning a woman spirit woke Kano Capoee and said that he would take many scalps during battles and would become a trusted counselor to the next village chief. While the boy talked to the spirit a giant salmon fish leaped out of the water, landed at the boy's feet and died. And then another fish, even larger than the first, leaped from the water to also die at the boy's feet. The boy ate parts of both animals, slept near the river that night, and returned to the village the next day. Kano Capoee told the elders about his vision and they renamed him Capoee Sorna, or Fish Spirits.

The young men walked proudly through the village arm in arm. Women with wagging tongues pointed at them and whispered. Old men lifted pipes from their mouths and nodded. Two girls walked past them and wiggled their bottoms. One of them, with hazel-colored eyes, long strong legs and small waist turned around and smiled at Nee Wahee. He smiled back and felt a strange stirring in his breast.

Wahee Na Tama Sorna

Nee Wahee returned to the council lodge just after the sun set. He coughed to let the elders know he was near, lifted the deerskin flap and entered. The elders were smoking pipes and sitting in a circle around a fire in the middle of the lodge. An opening in the circle had been left for him. Bright embers sputtered and glowed within the fire ring. Pungent odors of smoke from the fire blended with the sweet smell of pipe smoke and sharp body odors. The elders' eyes reflected orange of the embers, making them all seem like spirits to the young man.

He walked to the empty place in the circle and bowed to the elders. "Nee Wahee has come to hear you." His heart began beating faster because he knew that what the elders said would determine his future.

Smoke from the pipes curled around the elders' heads and covered the ceiling. Nee Wahee sneezed because there was so much smoke.

The senior member of the council, Hoa Nakoa, spoke. "Sit down Nee Wahee. You've had an eventful journey and wandered into places where even we would hesitate to go.

Your fight with the great bear left us breathless and we are grateful to your father for teaching you to be brave and to use your weapons well. We are pleased to have you home and in good health."

"Thank you. I'm very pleased to be home."

Hoa Nakoa continued speaking. "We believe your vision about the Spirits of the Mountains and that you will be important to the welfare of our people if they heed your advice. In fact, each of us has learned from your vision."

Hoa Nakoa handed Nee Wahee his long-stemmed pipe and the young man drew in smoke and filled his lungs without coughing. His heartbeats slowed.

After a lifetime, or so it seemed, Hoa Nakoa said, "We have named you Wahee Na Tama Sorna, or Bear of the Seven Spirits. We are honored to have you as a member of our village. Now go, and from this time forward act on the counsel that the Spirits of the Mountains gave you."

Wahee Na Tama Sorna turned toward the door and walked past his father. The chief stood and grabbed the young man by his arms. He said, "My son, I'm proud of you." They embraced, and both father and son wiped tears from their eyes.

El Viejo Leaves

The story is finished. I look at El Viejo and nod. "Thank you, Viejo. Now I know how the Seven Devils Mountains were named. I'll always feel the Spirits of the Mountains when I work in these mountains and in Hells Canyon."

"Remember the story and the counsel they gave to Nee Wahee as you pursue your own destiny. The advice must be followed as you continue your life." The old man takes out his pipe, stuffs it full of tobacco and lights it with a burning stick.

I bend over to stir the embers of the fire and glance up at El Viejo. "Did the spirits make it to the Upper World?"

"Si—yes, they went to the Upper World after the death of Wahee Na Tama Sorna because the chief had followed their advice and counsel during his lifetime and successfully led his people, and many people from other villages, through times of war and extreme hunger and cold."

The old man hesitates for several seconds and looks into the fire. He whispers, "The spirits come back now and then to visit these mountains and to help people who live and work near and in them."

El Viejo suddenly turns, smiles and stares into my eyes. "You don't know this, but the Spirits of the Mountains have helped when you were in grave danger while working in the canyon and among the Seven Devils Mountains. They also followed you on ships as you did your research, and to the islands on the north edge of the Pacific Ocean. Without their help you would not be alive. Can you recall seven near disasters that should have killed you?"

I think about my close calls with death during falls, forest fires, lightning strikes, rafting accidents, and animal encounters. I think about slipping on the deck of a rolling ship and nearly going overboard. I remember when a long cleat came off a research ship's gunwale during a rock-dredging procedure and struck me unconscious.

My arms sprout rigid hairs and my spine and neck tingle. I answer, "Yes, I know of at least seven."

El Viejo nods his head and whispers, "You must thank the Spirits of the Mountains for their protection."

"I'll do that whenever I remember."

"You should remember often."

I scrape the embers into a central cone within the fire ring, raise my eyebrows and glance at the old man. "Viejo, you said that you came on the back of an eagle and have lived a long time. I believe that you are a spirit and I know the story you told is true. In fact, Viejo, I believe you are one of the Spirits of the Mountains."

El Viejo smiles and says, "No, I'm not a Spirit of the Mountains."

I watch with amazement as El Viejo's body and facial features suddenly change and he becomes a young man. No wrinkles cut his cheeks and forehead and his lips part to reveal a full mouth of white teeth. His nose elongates and nostrils dilate. The yellow and gray eyes glitter as he stands on strong legs and walks toward a thick pine tree that grows on the edge of an embankment above Granite Creek. He turns back to face me as a tall warrior with broad shoulders and long white hair. Instead of denim, he now wears tight-fitting deerskin pants. He is shirtless and white scars stand out in stark contrast to the brown color of his shoulders. His eyes reflect the sunlight.

"You have no memory of it, but we met in your former life." The warrior raises his right hand in a salute, nods and then darts behind a large pine tree.

I think about that comment and wait several minutes for his return. Finally, I can wait no longer and walk around the pine tree. I search the creek and depths of the forest with my eyes. I call, "Viejo! Come back, Viejo!"

There is no reply.

Resounding flaps of giant wings startle me and I stare into the sky. An eagle is flying toward the peaks of the Seven Devils Mountains. It's the largest eagle I've ever seen.

The eagle turns and glides down the canyon past me. Something white is riding on its back. Goose bumps sprout on my arms and the back of my neck tingles. My heart beats so fast I can hardly breathe.

I yell, "Hello Kowamano! Hello Teacher Spirit of the Mountains!"

Kowamano banks and I clearly see the white object. It's a white wolf! I hold my breath, look more closely and stare into Lonoch Moro's eyes.

Acknowledgements

I gratefully acknowledge the inspiration provided by Paulo Coelho's book, *The Alchemist,* which I read several years ago. Some of his philosophy about destiny is included.

I appreciate the sketches made by Daniel A. Vallier, the careful editing by Jon Ytell, and the many suggestions for improvement by Sheila Canty-Vallier.

I thank family and friends, especially members of the Clifden Writing Group, for encouraging my writing efforts.

About the Author

Tracy Vallier lives with his wife Sheila in South Lake Tahoe, California and Clifden, Ireland. He retired in 1997 from the U.S. Geological Survey where he worked as a marine geologist. Since then, he taught at Lewis-Clark State College, Whitman College, and the University of Oregon and conducted research at Moss Landing Marine Laboratories. Tracy was born on a farm in western Iowa, but left soon after graduating from high school to join the U.S. Navy in order to receive the Korean G.I. Bill for a college education. He graduated from Iowa State University with a B.S. degree in geology and from Oregon State University with a Ph.D. in geology and oceanography. Tracy's scientific passion is the geology of Hells Canyon and neighboring Seven Devils Mountains where he has spent a large part of his career studying the geologic evolution of that region.

OTHER BOOKS

The Permian and Triassic Seven Devils Group, Western Idaho and Northeastern Oregon: U.S. Geological Survey Bulletin 1437, U.S. Government Printing Office, Washington, D.C., 1979.

Island and Rapids: A Geologic Story of Hells Canyon: Confluence Press, Lewiston, Idaho, 1998.

Conversations with an Idaho Bartender: Seven Devils Books, South Lake Tahoe, California, 2008.

Shadows in the Loess Hills: Seven Devils Books, South Lake Tahoe, California, 2009.